My favorite book, *Charlotte's Web*

My first web

Baby picture of me and Grampa

JUL 08

CH

For the girls—
Meghan, Jacqueline, Theresa,
Kerry, and Amanda
—D.C.

For Valerie
—H.B.

Library of Congress Cataloging-in-Publication Data   Cronin, Doreen.   Diary of a spider / by Doreen Cronin ; pictures by Harry Bliss.—1st ed.   p. cm.   Summary: A young spider discovers, day by day, that there is a lot to learn about being a spider, including how to spin webs and avoid vacuum cleaners.   ISBN 0-06-000153-4   —   ISBN 0-06-000154-2 (lib. bdg.)   [1. Spiders—Fiction.   2. Insects—Fiction.   3. Diaries—Fiction.]   I. Bliss, Harry, 1964- ill.   II. Title.   PZ7.C88133Dg 2005   2004011549   [E]—dc22   Typography by Alicia Mikles   1 2 3 4 5 6 7 8 9 10   ❖   First Edition

By Doreen Cronin • Pictures by Harry Bliss

DIARY OF A SPIDER

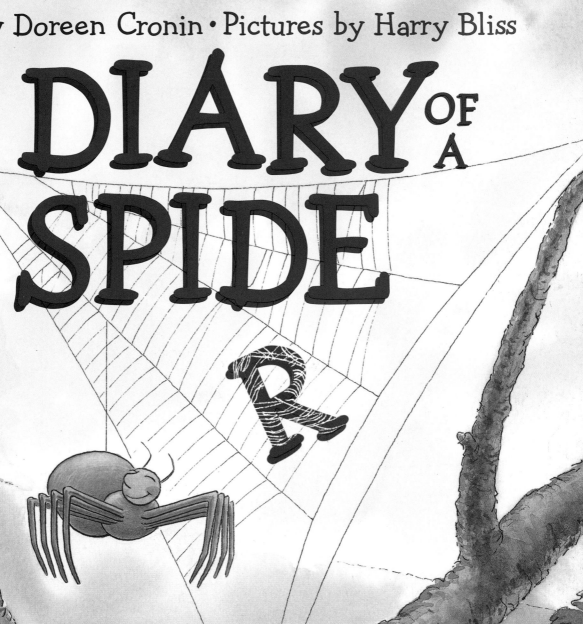

JOANNA COTLER BOOKS
An Imprint of HarperCollinsPublishers

Today was Grandparents Day at school, so I brought Grampa with me.

He taught us three things:

1. Spiders are not insects—insects have six legs.

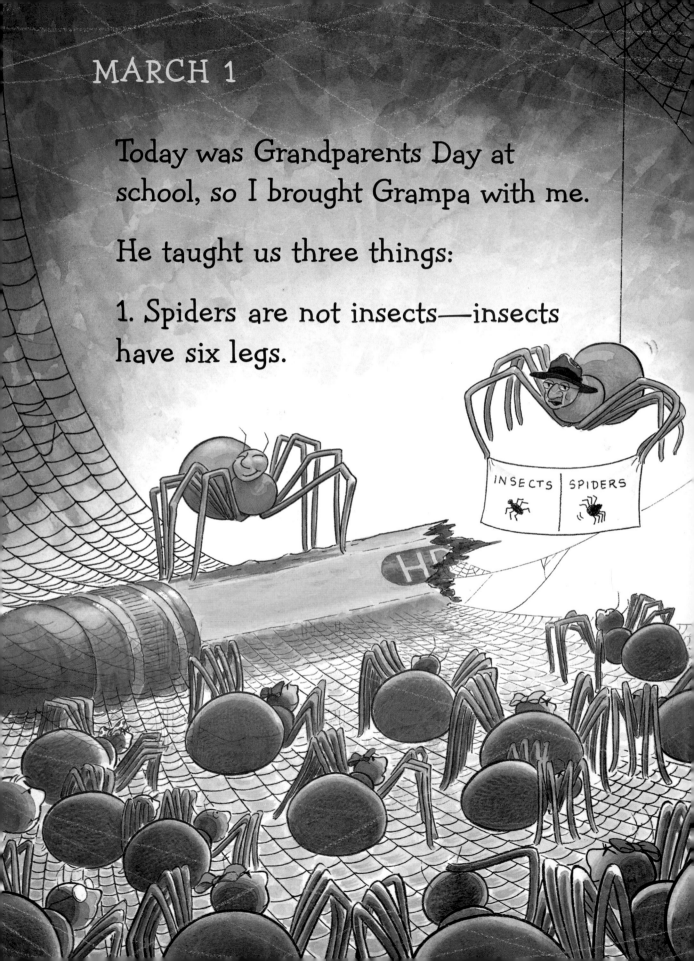

2. Without spiders, insects could take over the world.

3. Butterflies taste better with a little barbecue sauce.

MARCH 16

Grampa says that in his day, flies and spiders did not get along.

The Compost Tim

THURSDAY APRIL 16 1971

Spiders and Flies Rumble in the City

Trash mouth!

Cannibal!

BY THE ASSOCIATED WEB

An ordinary Friday night in town turned ugly when Spiders and Flies squared off against each other in a fierce battle. Web-slinging insults of the most gruesome sort were reported from all over the metropolitan "I've never heard such horrible name-calling in all my life," said "I nearly broke a wing trying to fly outta there—it was ...issioner Ed Grasshopper has closed Rubbish "It's troubling for the future of

MARCH 29

Today in gym class we learned how to catch the wind so we could travel to faraway places.

When I got home, I made up flash cards so I could practice:

1. Climb high.

2. Release silk.

3. Catch wind.

Fly made up her own flash card:

1. Fly.

I'm starting to see why Grampa doesn't like her.

APRIL 1

Went to the park with my sister today.
We tried the seesaw.

It didn't work.

We tried the tire swing.

It didn't work.

We spun a huge sticky web
on the water fountain.

That worked.

EEEEEEK!

APRIL 12

Today was Safety Day at school. We learned that vacuums eat spiderwebs and are very, very dangerous. If we hear a vacuum, we should Stop, Drop, and Run.

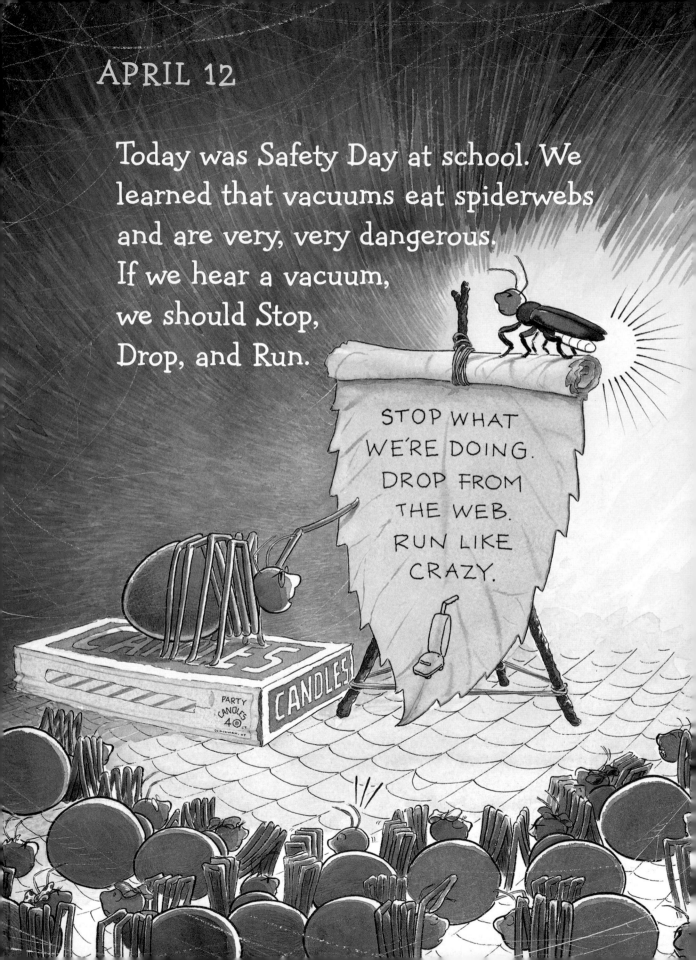

STOP WHAT WE'RE DOING. DROP FROM THE WEB. RUN LIKE CRAZY.

APRIL 13

We had a vacuum drill today.
I stopped what I was doing.

Forgot where I was going.

And ran screaming from the room.

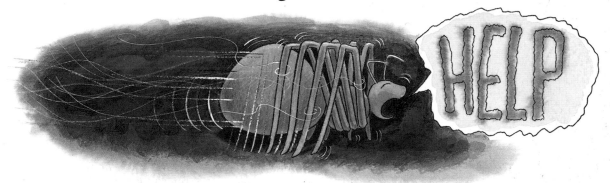

We're having another drill tomorrow.

APRIL 17

I'm sleeping over at Worm's house tonight.

I hope they don't have leaves and rotten tomatoes for dinner again.

MAY 8

Today was show-and-tell.
So I brought in my old skin.

My teacher called on it to
lead the Pledge of Allegiance.

JUNE 5

Daddy Longlegs made fun of Fly because she eats with her feet. Now she won't come out of her tree house.

I'm going to find him and give him a piece of my mind!

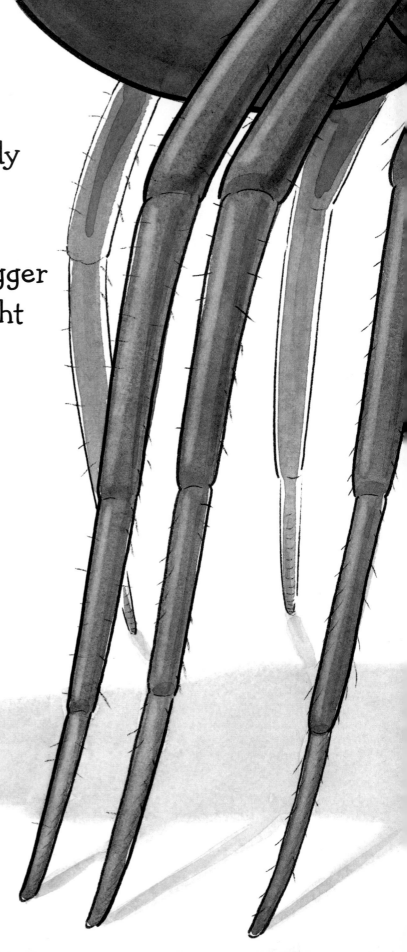

JUNE 6

I found Daddy
Longlegs.

He's a lot bigger
than I thought
he was.

I gave him a piece
of my lunch
instead.

JUNE 7

Fly's tree house blew away
in the wind today.

So did Grampa.

JUNE 18

I got a postcard from Grampa today:

Dear Spider,
Ooh-la-la!
I landed in Paris!
French bugs are
delicious!
Au revoir,
Grampa

leg
of
French
gnat...
give it a try!

PARIS · FRANCE

Spider
5 Web Ave.
Arachnidville
05400
USA

Tanet co.

JUNE 30

Grampa came home today.

I couldn't wait to hear about
how he rode the winds
all the way over the ocean!

Turns out, he caught a breeze to the
airport and napped in first class.

JULY 2

Fly came over to play today. She got stuck in our web, and her mom had to come get her.

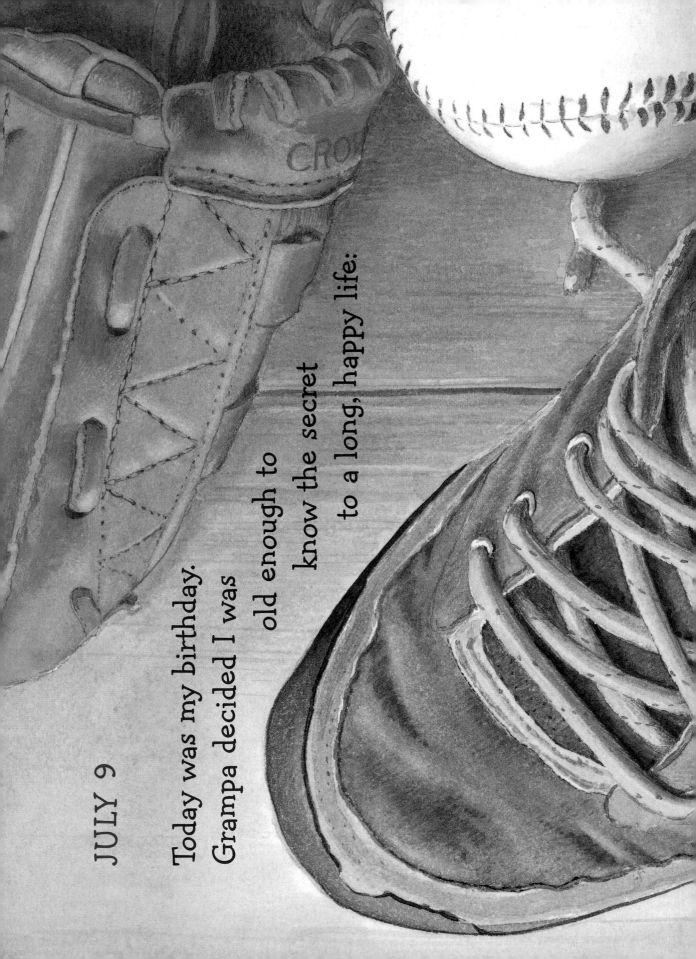

JULY 9

Today was my birthday.
Grampa decided I was
old enough to
know the secret
to a long, happy life:

Never fall asleep in a shoe.

JULY 16

Things I scare:

1. Fly's mom

2. Tiny bugs

3. People using water fountains at the park

JULY 17

Things that scare me:

1. Daddy Longlegs

2. Vacuums

3. People with big feet

AUGUST 1

I wish that people wouldn't judge all spiders based on the few spiders that bite.

SPIDER'S CLUBHOUSE

FORTIFIED

VITAMIN C

ALL NATURAL

I know if we took the time to get to know each other, we would get along just fine.

Just like me and Fly.

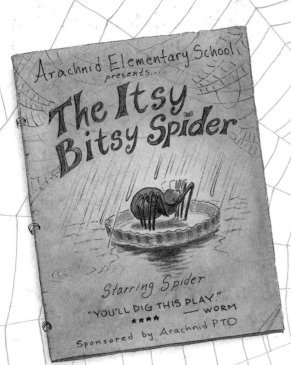

Dad made me this!

Worm found this!